D1126789

COPING IN A CHANGING WORLD

STRESS

Linda Bickerstaf

ROSEN
PUBLISHING®

New York

Published in 2007 by The Rosen Publishing Group, Inc.
29 East 21st Street, New York, NY 10010

First Edition

Library of Congress Cataloging-in-Publication Data

Bickerstaff, Linda.
Stress / Linda Bickerstaff.
    p. cm.—(Coping in a changing world)
ISBN-13: 978-1-4042-0951-0
ISBN-10: 1-4042-0951-4 (library binding)
1. Stress in adolescence. 2. Stress management for
teenagers. I. Title.
BF724.3.S86B53 2006
155.5'18—dc22

                                                2006024422

Printed in China

Contents

CHAPTER ONE

Defining Stress

STRESS OVERLOAD THAT IS IGNORED OR HANDLED INCORRECTLY CAN RESULT IN SERIOUS PHYSICAL AND EMOTIONAL PROBLEMS.

Your parents might say that stress is working hard enough to keep bread on the table, pay the mortgage, and put aside a little money for college tuition. A coach might tell you that stress is losing the championship game by one point in double overtime. Your best friend might say that stress is taking the SAT exams the day after the prom!

In his article "The Nature of Stress," Dr. Hans Selye says that stress occurs when demands, or stressors, are made on us and our bodies respond with a series of changes. The changes lead to what is called the stress response. A stress response enhances a person's ability to perform well under the pressure of whatever stressor initiates it.[1]

We are surrounded by multitudes of stressors that trigger stress responses. At times, these occur so closely together that our bodies are constantly stressed—a condition called stress overload. It is important to find ways to minimize stress overload or, if that is unavoidable, to deal with it productively. Stress overload that is ignored or handled incorrectly can result in serious physical and emotional problems.

WHO GETS STRESSED?

Everyone is bombarded by stressors and has stress reactions on a daily basis. However, stress and stress responses are not necessarily negative events. They help us to respond to changes that we encounter and that make life worth living.

However, many stressors can be overwhelming and may lead to stressed-out feelings. Most adults admit to being stressed out at times, but many have the mistaken impression that teens are stress-free and certainly never stressed out. Nothing could be further from the truth. Teen stressors may be different from adult stressors, but that does not make them any less real.

THE HISTORY OF STRESS

The word "stress" was coined and the nature of stress was understood when two physicians, Walter Bradford Cannon (1871–1945) and Hans Selye (1907–1982), began to publish the results of their research efforts.

Cannon started medical school at Harvard University in 1896. He was very interested in physiology, the study of how living organisms function. During medical school, he did much research on how food moves through the esophagus, stomach, and intestines—a process called peristalsis. Peristalsis results when the smooth muscles of the stomach and intestines contract rhythmically to push food along the digestive system. He observed that peristalsis was greatly diminished if a person was in great pain, had been badly frightened, or was very angry. When a person was again pain-free or serene, peristalsis returned to normal.

In his autobiography, *The Way of an Investigator*, Dr. Cannon said it suddenly occurred to him that feelings such as pain, fright, and anger affected peristalsis and other bodily functions for a reason. He theorized that when presented with severe stress, the body shuts down certain functions, like digestion, which aren't needed in life-or-death situations. By doing this, the body can move blood to parts of the body, including the brain, heart, lungs, and muscles, where it is needed immediately.[2] Thus, the concept of the fight-or-flight response was born. Dr. Cannon spent years studying the many changes that occur in a body under stress and amplified the concept of the fight-or-flight response. He published his findings in *Bodily Changes in Pain, Hunger, Fear and Rage*, in 1915.[3]

MARY'S STORY

Mary was not happy to be herding her grand-mother's sheep to spring pasture. As a young girl, she had loved to spend time with her grandmother and was thrilled to hear her grand-mother's stories of encounters with bears or fighting off eagles who swooped down to carry off newborn lambs. Now that she was older, Mary found herding sheep was hot, dirty, boring work.

Mary had just moved the sheep into a deep canyon where fresh grass grew when she sensed she was being watched. This is crazy, she thought. I'm the only one out here. But the feeling persisted. Just then, a small pebble bounced down the red face of the canyon wall in front of her.

Though she was not aware of it, in a split second her heart rate and blood pressure soared. She began to breathe rapidly, sending oxygen to her brain and muscles, and the pupils of her eyes dilated to improve her vision. Her liver poured glucose (sugar) into her bloodstream to provide energy so she could fight or flee if necessary. But it wasn't necessary. As she looked up at a ledge on the canyon wall far above, she saw a cougar dragging a small deer. The cougar soundlessly disappeared into a rock fissure.

Mary's heart rate took several minutes to return to normal, but by then she was already leading her reluctant sheep out of the canyon. Maybe sheepherding wasn't so boring after all— and maybe her grandmother's stories were not just figments of her imagination!

DR. STRESS

Dr. Hans Selye was known as "Dr. Stress" in medical circles because of his contributions to the understanding of the effects of stress on humans. He started medical school in 1925, ten years after Dr. Cannon described the fight-or-flight response. Dr. Selye's research, which he began in medical school and continued throughout the rest of his life, supported Dr. Cannon's views. He showed that stimuli, which he called stressors, cause the same body reactions seen in the fight-or-flight response proposed by Dr. Cannon. Dr. Cannon may have introduced the terms "stress" and "stress reaction," but Dr. Selye popularized the word and the concept.

Dr. Selye also differentiated between good stress and bad stress. Good stress, which he called eustress, is comprised of bodily responses to stressors that help protect us in times of danger. Eustress gears us up to study for exams, helps us to meet deadlines, and keeps us on our toes in order to meet life's challenges. Eustress allows our bodies to return to an unstressed state within a short interval of time.

Bad stress, which Dr. Selye called distress, is the result of too much of a good thing. Stress responses are automatic, and people can do nothing to prevent them from occurring. If a person is constantly being stressed, his or her body's stress reactions will begin to overlap. Temporary bodily changes, like elevated blood pressure and heart rate, may be present all of the time. This can contribute to the development of very significant health problems, including heart attacks and strokes.

Dr. Cannon and Dr. Selye paved the way for the study of the effects of stress on our bodies and minds—probably not realizing how important their work would be in an increasingly stressful world. We will see how the observations they made and the groundwork they laid have been used by present-day scientists to help us cope with stress.

CHAPTER TWO

Body Talk:
The Physiology
of Stress

*EACH OF US HAS A UNIQUE
SET OF STRESSORS.*

You cannot go through a day of your life without stressors and reacting to them. Regardless of what the stressor is, your body will react the same way every time it is stressed. The following is a list of the major changes that occur in the body when it is stressed. Prolonged or chronic stress may lead to more serious changes that will be discussed later.

- A person's heart rate, respiratory rate, and blood pressure increase in response to stress. At the same time, blood flow to the skin, digestive system, and kidneys decreases. As a result, more blood is shunted to organs, like the lungs, brain, and large muscle groups, that really need it in emergency situations. By increasing respiratory rate and blood flow to the lungs, more oxygen can be picked up and carried to other organs. When blood flow is increased to the brain, its ability to respond quickly to stressors improves. Increased blood flow to large muscle groups enables you to flee from a perceived danger.
- Sweating increases during stressful situations. The chemical reactions occurring in the body in response to stress create a lot of body heat. Increased sweating helps the body eliminate this extra heat.
- The pupils of a person's eyes dilate, or enlarge, as a response to stress. When the pupils dilate, they allow more light into the eyes to improve vision.

- Stored glycogen is released from the liver of an acutely stressed person. When undergoing a stress reaction, the body needs a lot of extra energy to fuel its systems. The body's energy source is glucose, a form of sugar. The liver, which stores sugar as glycogen, releases it in response to stress.

- Stress causes the release of stored platelets and clotting factors. If you cut your finger, platelets, small particles that circulate in the bloodstream, cause a chemical reaction that makes your blood clot at the site of the cut. In a stress reaction, large numbers of platelets, which are stored in the marrow of our bones, are sent out into the circulating blood. At the same time, chemicals called clotting factors, which are also necessary for blood clotting, are shunted out of storage into the bloodstream to speed up the clotting mechanism if it is needed.

A DOMINO EFFECT

Let's examine a hypothetical scenario to look at the domino effect of a stress reaction. Imagine that you're deep in thought about an upcoming date. You step off a curb without looking both ways and don't see a car that is traveling down the street. You are wrenched from your thoughts by the sound of screeching brakes. Here is what happens:

1. The screech of the brakes travels to your ears, where it causes your eardrums to

vibrate. The vibrations are carried by the three bones of the middle ear to nerve cells in your inner ears. There, they are converted to electrical impulses. These impulses are carried by your auditory nerves to your brain.

2. The impulses travel deep into the brain to the hypothalamus. Here, cells begin to make a hormone called corticotropin-releasing hormone (CRH).

3. CRH is dumped into the blood and carried through small veins to your pituitary gland, which is located outside the brain just below the hypothalamus. Once it reaches the pituitary gland, CRH acts on its cells and causes them to make another hormone called adrenocorticotropin hormone (ACTH).

4. ACTH is then absorbed into the blood and carried all the way from the head to the adrenal glands, two clumps of tissue located just above the kidneys. There, ACTH causes cells of the adrenal glands to produce three hormones: cortisol, epinephrine, and norepinephrine.

5. The three hormones made by the adrenal glands travel through the bloodstream to different places in your body. Cortisol goes to your liver, where it pushes glucose that is stored there into the blood. The glucose is then carried to organs that need it. Epinephrine and norepinephrine travel all over your body to stimulate your autonomic nervous system. This system is made up of nerves that are

found in the organs themselves. When epinephrine stimulates the autonomic nervous system in the heart, for instance, your heart rate soars. Epinephrine also causes your respiratory rate to increase and your blood pressure to go up.

After you scramble back onto the curb unharmed, your stress reaction begins to subside. The reaction is turned off when you no longer need all the cortisol your adrenal glands are producing. The extra cortisol is carried back to the brain where it stops the hypothalamus from producing CRH. This is called a feedback mechanism, and it is one of the ways the body turns off reactions it no longer needs.

STRESS RESPONSES MAY VARY

Dr. George Chrousos, chief of the Pediatric and Reproductive Endocrinology Branch of the National Institute of Child Health and Human Development (NICHD), believes that stress responses vary from person to person. If two people are subjected to the same stressor, each will initiate the same responses. However, these responses may be expressed differently.

For instance, if two teens are taking the same test, each will have an increase in heart rate and blood pressure. The student who did not study hard enough will probably have a much higher heart rate and higher blood pressure than the student who did. Once the stressor is gone, the stress response is switched off. According to Dr. Chrousos, a person's genetic makeup may influence his or her stress response. Some may fail to have strong enough responses to a threat, while others over-respond to even minor stressors. Each of these variants can lead to long-term health problems.

Dr. Chrousos also says that extreme stress at any given time in your life can alter your brain's hormone production, leading to one extreme of response or the other. Major stress in early childhood is especially likely to alter stress responses. If young children experience extreme stress, they may overreact to even minor stress when they grow up.[1]

GENERAL ADAPTATION SYNDROME

Hans Selye certainly earned the nickname of Dr. Stress. Through his laboratory research and his lifelong observation of stressed people, he discovered that stress causes a three-stage pattern of response, which he called the general adaptation syndrome (GAD).[2] He called these three stages the alarm stage, the adaptive/resistance stage, and the exhaustion stage.

The alarm stage is the stage you exhibited when you stepped off the curb. You sensed a threat and your body responded to allow you to get back to the curb unharmed. After the car passed, your body's stress reaction was turned off and your physiologic parameters, like heart rate and blood pressure, started to return to normal.

As you continue your walk down the street, you again hear screeching brakes. Although you are no longer in harm's way, you experience another stress reaction. However, your heart rate and blood pressure are not as high as with your first reaction. This is what Dr. Selye called the adaptive/resistance stage in his general adaptation syndrome.

People who experience unrelenting stress may reach the point where they can no longer mount a stress response. Dr. Selye labeled this the exhaustion stage of his general adaptation syndrome.

RECOGNIZING STRESS

Each of us has a unique set of stressors. You may find that giving a speech is extremely stressful, while playing a solo in a band concert is not. Your best friend may have just the opposite response to these two stressors. Every person also has unique ways of responding in stressful situations. When you have to give a speech, for instance, you may develop a very dry mouth and a tight throat that make it almost impossible to talk. Your friend, on the other hand, has no trouble speaking but may break out in a sweat. It is helpful to be tuned in to how you respond to stress. Some of your responses may be so subtle that you may not recognize them as stress responses at first.

Some of the more common physical signs that you may experience in a stressful situation include a pounding heart, a tight or dry throat, chest pain, indigestion, headache, cold or sweaty hands, difficulty sleeping, and extreme fatigue.

Psychological signs of stress can include anxiety, irritability, depression, a feeling of helplessness or hopelessness, sadness, apathy, or anger. When we are stressed out, we frequently exhibit unusual and sometimes destructive types of behavior, like overeating or not eating at all. Some people become argumentative or abusive, neglect their personal hygiene, withdraw from friends, or start performing poorly in school. Some may even go as far as to start using drugs or alcohol.

Recognizing your unique stressors and how you respond to them, as well as understanding what is really happening in your body when you are stressed, are the first steps in learning to control stress.

CHAPTER THREE

Stress-Related Illness

TALKING WITH YOUR SCHOOL NURSE OR COUNSELOR MIGHT BE THE FIRST STEP IN LEARNING TO HANDLE YOUR STRESS.

nyone who has ever experienced stress overload can tell you how miserable it can make you feel. Dr. Chrousos and others who work with people who are stressed know that if the stress cycle cannot be turned off, stress reactions can be very harmful. The authors of an article from the National Institutes of Health (NIH), "Stress System Malfunction Could Lead to Serious, Life-Threatening Disease," said:

> In our modern society, stress doesn't always let up. Many of us now harbor anxiety and worry about daily events and relationships. Stress hormones continue to wash through the system in high levels, never leaving the blood and tissue. . . . Research now shows that such long-term activation of the stress system can have a hazardous, even lethal effect on the body, increasing risk of obesity, heart disease, depression, and a variety of other illnesses.[1]

NEGATIVE EFFECTS OF STRESS

Dr. Selye called stress-related maladies "diseases of adaptation" because they occur in people who cannot adapt to stress. He listed the most common ones: ulcers of the stomach and upper small intestine, hypertension (high blood pressure), heart attacks, and various disturbances of the nervous system.[2] Let's look at how stress contributes to these and other illnesses or disorders that we encounter.

Peptic Ulcer

A peptic ulcer is an area in the stomach or the first portion of the small intestine, the duodenum, where the normal lining of these organs, the mucosa, has been worn away. This hole in the mucosa allows the contents of the stomach, which contain a large amount of acid, to penetrate into the underlying muscles. Occasionally, ulcers will penetrate not only through the mucosa but also through the muscular walls of the stomach or duodenum. If that happens, food and acid spill into the abdominal cavity, usually with catastrophic, potentially life-threatening results.

During Dr. Selye's time, it was thought that ulcers were caused by two things that commonly occurred in people who were under a lot of stress: the production of too much acid by the stomach and slow emptying of acid and food from the stomach. Years before Dr. Selye started to work, Dr. Cannon had shown that stress decreased gastric and duodenal peristalsis. Dr. Selye observed the same thing and felt that stress played a significant role in the development of ulcers. While Dr. Selye's observation about the high frequency of peptic ulcers in overstressed people was correct, the reasons he proposed for the development of ulcers were not.

Current knowledge about the formation of peptic ulcers centers around a bacterium called

Helicobacter pylori. H. pylori is a very common bacterium that many people harbor in their bodies. People with peptic ulcers have been shown to have large quantities of *H. pylori* in their stomachs. It is theorized that severe stress decreases a person's ability to fight infections by decreasing immune responses. *H. pylori* may multiply in the stomachs of these individuals because their immune systems cannot fight the bacteria off. As a result, they develop ulcers.

There are many factors other than stress that contribute to ulcer formation, but inability to cope with stress compounds the problem. The upset stomach you may occasionally get when you are worried about taking a test is not a symptom of the development of an ulcer. On the other hand, if stress controls your life and you do not find productive ways to cope with it, you might be setting yourself up for problems. Talking with your school nurse or counselor might be the first step in learning to handle your stress.

Hypertension

Hypertension (high blood pressure) contributes to the development of heart attacks and strokes. According to the *Merck Manual of Diagnosis and Therapy*, at least fifty million Americans are hypertensive.[3]

Hypertension is one of the main culprits in the development of atherosclerosis (hardening of the arteries), which can lead to heart attacks and strokes. Combined, heart attacks and strokes are the number-one killer of people in the United States.[4]

You already know that the epinephrine released in stress responses causes elevations in blood pressure and heart rate. In stress overload, large amounts of epinephrine are present in the circulatory system all the time. This causes very high blood pressure, especially in people who have inherited the tendency to develop hypertension. People who are overweight or who have high cholesterol levels are also at special risk to develop hypertension.

As blood rushes through arteries at high pressures, the inner lining of the arteries, the intima, becomes damaged. In an attempt to repair the arteries, the body lays down additional layers of intimal cells, causing the intima to thicken and the lumens to narrow. Over time, blood flow through these narrowing, inflexible vessels slows. If the flow gets slow enough, blood clots form, blocking the vessel entirely. When this occurs in an artery that supplies blood to the heart muscle itself, the part of the heart being supplied with blood by that vessel will die because it will not get oxygen. This leads to what is known as a heart attack, or myocardial infarction. If many heart muscles die, a heart attack is usually fatal.

The same thing can happen in the arteries carrying blood to the brain or to arteries in the brain itself. If brain tissue loses its blood supply, it will die. This results in a cerebral vascular accident, or stroke. A person who has a massive stroke may die. Less massive strokes can lead to severe speech impairments or loss of use of extremities. While the brain can sometimes repair itself or reroute nerve impulses, most people who have major strokes never fully recover.

Obesity

Obesity is a national epidemic. Over the last several decades, lifestyles have changed drastically in the United States. People, including most teens, are eating a lot of fast food, which contains huge numbers of calories. We also are exercising less than we used to. As a result, our caloric intakes are exceeding our caloric expenditures, so we are getting fatter. If you add stress to the mix, you compound the problem. People who are stressed out produce large amounts of cortisol. Cortisol is known to increase appetite, so when we are stressed, we are hungrier and eat more. Eating at night is especially common in people who are under a lot of stress.

Dr. Rebecca Moran, in an article entitled "Evaluation and Treatment of Childhood Obesity," says that 25 to 30 percent of U.S. children are obese. Over the last ten years, the incidence of obesity has increased almost 40 percent in those between the ages of twelve and seventeen. Although the main causes of this epidemic of obesity in teens are the same as with adults, Dr. Moran thinks the high stress levels that teens experience are contributing to the problem. One of the negative coping mechanisms seen in stressed-out teens is overeating.[5]

Depression

Some types of depression are characterized by anxiety, rapid heart rate, and high blood pressure, among other things. Do these signs sound familiar? These are the same signs found in stress reactions. In this disorder, the problem appears to be that the feedback mechanism for turning off CRH does not work. People who develop depression when overstressed may do so because they are genetically programmed to produce too much CRH. In an apparent attempt to turn off CRH production, these people produce a lot of cortisol. One of the side effects of having high levels of cortisol in your blood is depression.

While not all types of depression are associated with high cortisol levels, depression is a frequent symptom seen in kids who are stressed out. When they feel that they can no longer cope with a stressful situation, some kids think the only option is to escape from the situation by committing suicide. In the May 1995 issue of the *Canadian Journal of Continuing Medical Education*, Maurice Blackman, clinical professor and director of the Division of Child and Adolescent Psychiatry at the University of Alberta Hospitals, Alberta, Canada, presented some alarming statistics. He reported that the suicide rate for adolescents has increased more than

200 percent over the last decade. Adolescent suicide is now responsible for more deaths in teenagers age fifteen to nineteen than cardiovascular disease or cancer.[6] This increase in today's suicide rate reflects the increase in depression seen in the teens, as well as the increased levels of teen stress.

Immune System

The body's immune system has the responsibility of protecting it from foreign invaders such as bacteria or viruses. When the immune system kicks into gear, immune molecules are made in various cells of the system to coordinate an attack on foreign invaders.

Immune molecules can activate the hypothalamus, starting a typical stress reaction that results in the production of cortisol by the adrenal glands. Cortisol actually has the effect of making immune cells less effective in fighting invaders. In overstressed people, high levels of cortisol are circulating all the time. As a result, their immune systems don't work effectively and they are more susceptible to colds, the flu, or other infections. How many times have you developed a fever blister or cold sore on your lip just before a big event like the prom? These irritating and unsightly lesions are symptoms of herpes simplex, which is caused by a virus that can lie dormant in nerve tissue for years. Physical or emotional stress with immune system suppression is one of the most common causes of a new outcropping of blisters.

OTHER STRESS-RELATED PHYSICAL PROBLEMS

George Chrousos and Phillip Gold, both clinicians and researchers at the NIH, have worked for the past twenty years to understand the effects of unrelenting stress on the human body. The following are some of the effects that they have observed.

Stress may keep the reproductive system from functioning correctly. Teens who are significantly stressed out have high amounts of cortisol circulating in their bloodstreams. In girls, this keeps ovaries from releasing eggs, and in boys, it keeps testes from releasing sperm. The production of testosterone, estrogen, and progesterone (sex hormones) is also impaired. Adult ballerinas and long-distance runners are examples of people in whom physical stress is common. These individuals, like teens with significant stress, are also known to have very high circulating cortisol levels. They have reproductive system malfunctions that can last for several years after they cease dancing or running.[7]

Prolonged activation of the hypothalamus may keep the pituitary gland from secreting the hormone needed for normal growth. Children who are emotionally and physically abused at a young age can experience growth retardation—a condition called psychosocial short stature syndrome. Their pituitary glands are producing a lot of ACTH in response to stress at the expense of the production of growth hormone. If they are placed in caring environments and receive sufficient positive attention, thereby reducing their stress levels, their growth will resume.

These are just a few examples of the effects of stress and overstress on the body. Cases like these prove that too much stress can lead to diseases and disorders that can not only shorten life but also make the process of living difficult.

CHAPTER FOUR

Teen Stress

Almost 70 percent of teens reported that they had major stressors related to school issues.

D r. Jannie Carter, in her article "Teens 2003: Have We Really Been There and Done That?," reaffirms a fact that will come as no surprise to you. Most adults don't think of teens as being stressed, and yet the teen years—years during which you are making major physical and emotional transitions—are filled with stressful situations that would test the coping skills of any adult.[1]

DO ALL TEENS FEEL STRESSED OUT?

Several agencies and organizations have conducted surveys of various teen populations to get real data on how stressed teens are, what issues are most stressful for them, and what they are doing about these issues. While all of these surveys sought information, the purpose of gathering the information varied with the organization conducting them. The questions asked in each survey were therefore varied, but one question was universal to all of them: "Are you stressed out?" The answer universally was "yes."

In December 2003 and again in November 2004, Mediamark Research, Inc., a leading provider of multimedia consumer research data, conducted the MRI Teenmark survey. Each survey involved about 4,500 teens between the ages of twelve and nineteen. The results of the 2004 survey and a comparison of the two surveys were published on November 24, 2004, in an article entitled "Teens Want to Enjoy Life and Relationships, Not Climb the Corporate Ladder." One finding of both surveys was that 51 percent of the responders felt stressed out "all of the time" or at least "sometimes," while only 2 percent said they were never stressed. More girls (60 percent) said they were stressed than boys (50 percent).[2]

In another survey conducted at Marlborough High School in Marlborough, Massachusetts, and reported October, 16, 2002, in the *Milford Daily News*, a whopping 70 percent of the 815 teens who responded said they were stressed out.[3] As you might expect, teens share some stressors with both adults and with younger kids, but they have a few stressors that are unique to them.

DOES EVERYONE HAVE THE SAME STRESSORS?

To a large extent, stressors are age-related. In January 2006, the American Psychological Association conducted a telephone survey of 2,152 adults eighteen years of age or older. The results of that survey were reported in an article, "Americans Engage in Unhealthy Behaviors to Manage Stress." Money and work issues were stressors for 60 percent of the adults surveyed, while about 50 percent said that health issues, either personal or those of family members, were major concerns. Worries about their children stressed 41 percent of adults. Over half of those surveyed said that the state of world affairs was stressful to them.[4] Teens, as we will see, share many of these same concerns, although most are not in the top-ten list of teen stressors.

Adolescents and younger teens between the ages of nine and thirteen share many stressors with older teens, but they have a few that are unique to their age group. A survey reported by Georgia Witkin in her book *KidStress* and a second conducted by the Nemours Foundation KidsHealth Web site showed similar results. These two surveys asked 1,800 kids about their levels of stress and the things that caused them stress. As many as 84 percent of kids said they worried some of the time, and a few placed themselves in a "stressed out" category.[5, 6]

Getting good grades in school was the biggest stressor for this group, followed closely by family concerns (discord between parents and conflicts with siblings). Over a third of the group reported that peer-pressure issues such as teasing, bullying, and "fickle" friends were stressors. Like adults, kids worry about national and international problems. Environmental concerns, the possibility of more terrorist attacks, and even the possibility of nuclear war were stressors for about one-third of those in this group. You don't have to be a teen to worry about your future or your appearance. About 40 percent of those in the nine-to-thirteen age group worried about whether they would qualify for a good college, make enough money to support a family, and find the "right" mate. An equal number were stressed by appearance concerns including their weight, skin, and hair.

TEEN STRESSORS

Though teens share stressors with adults and younger kids, what are the stressors that are most bothersome to them? Are there any stressors that are unique to teens? To answer those questions, we can combine data from the following three surveys. The results of these surveys were almost identical.

Forty teens at the West Arkansas Church of Christ were surveyed in 1998 about their top three stressors, and they gave very candid answers to the questions that they were asked. A year later, a large survey was conducted by the Boys and Girls Clubs of America in conjunction with the Taco Bell Foundation and was reported in an article entitled "17,000 Teens Speak Out Through Landmark National Survey." Data from these surveys, combined with that from the MRI Teenmark survey previously mentioned, give the opinions of more than 20,000 teens on the subject of stress and stressors.

Major teen stressors fall into three categories, all of which appear to be of equal importance. The first of these are stressors caused by the relationship of teens with their parents. More than half of the 20,000 teens polled in the combined surveys said they had major stress issues with their parents. Some said they were stressed because they were seemingly never able to please their parents. Others said their parents gave them little, if any, freedom and always had to be in control. Other teens reported that their parents put tremendous pressure on them to succeed—a very stressful situation when what constitutes success to a parent might not mean the same thing to a teen.

Peer-pressure stressors are also very real to teens. Included in this category are stressors emerging from relationships. About 30 percent of teens had significant stress problems in their relationships (boyfriends and girlfriends), many stemming from differences of opinion about sexual matters. Fitting or not fitting into particular groups (cliques, clubs, gangs, and sororities/fraternities) also created stress for about 30 percent of teens. Included in this category of stressors were issues of appearance, like wearing fashionable clothes or being overweight. Many teens reported that they were stressed when pressured by their peers to smoke, drink, and use drugs.

Almost 70 percent of teens reported that they had major stressors related to school issues. Getting good grades was still a stressor for teens, but it was a minor stressor compared to the perceived need of being "all things to all people." Teens reported being especially stressed by knowing that they were not only expected to get good grades but were also expected to participate in a variety of activities, to excel at sports, to be student leaders, and to even work part-time.[7, 8, 9]

MIKE'S STORY

The light over Mike's desk was still on at 3 AM. He was incredibly tired but could not sleep—he

*simply couldn't turn off his thoughts. He knew
that if he slowed down, he would only get further behind.*

*Mike had to plan his entire day if he hoped
to get everything done. Unfortunately, he felt as
though he barely had enough time to breathe or
go to the bathroom. It is a pretty sad state of
affairs, he thought, when you actually have to set
aside a few minutes to be with your girlfriend.*

*He had made it to school by 7 AM. Things
went pretty well with his four morning classes,
even the pop quiz Mr. Loftin gave in physics. At
noon, he met with the student council to argue
for more student parking, quickly ate his lunch,
returned a library book, and still made his cal-
culus class at 1 PM. Fortunately for his crowded
schedule, the long jump was held early in the
intercity track meet that afternoon. He was
really dragging because he hadn't slept much the
night before. His jumps weren't spectacular. In
fact, according to his coach, they were pitiful—
not a real ego booster. By the time Mike showered,
the hour he had set aside to be with his girlfriend had shrunk to thirty minutes.*

*Mike's two-hour work shift at the YMCA was
frantic. Almost every member had either lost a
locker key, forgotten a towel, or couldn't get the
TV in the weight room to work. Mike finally got
home at 7:30 PM. His mom was angry because
he was supposed to be home at seven o'clock to
babysit his little brothers so she could help with
a catering job. After getting them to bed and*

eating a quick sandwich, he finally got started on his application for the SAT exams. By this time it was 10 PM, and Mike could barely keep his eyes open. "If the SATs are as bad as the application forms," he said to himself, "I'm in big trouble."

His mother got home at 11 PM and wanted to have a talk with him. Their discussion—centered around Mike setting a better example for his brothers, taking more responsibility, and volunteering to help with the kids at an upcoming school carnival—ended at about midnight.

He started on his homework shortly thereafter. He needed to go to sleep, but he was listening to his mind rattle on and on and on. Why couldn't he just shut it off? Had he finally reached the end of his rope? It certainly felt like it.

CHAPTER FIVE

Major Teen Stressors

NO FAMILY SITUATION IS STRESS-FREE.

S tatistics support the fact that most teens are significantly stressed, at least part of the time. While each person has his or her own set of major stressors, there is a group of stressors that appears to be common to most teens. Family issues, illness, school, peer-group pressures, and global issues can have a significant effect on a teen's life. The following discussions show that many teens are definitely going through the same issues as you are.

FAMILY ISSUES

No family situation is stress-free. Even teens who are lucky enough to have caring parents and reasonable siblings are sometimes stressed by family issues. They know, however, that they can rely on family members for support. Some teens are not so lucky. The following stressors are among the hardest that teens deal with.

Abuse

Abuse is an underreported source of stress for many teens. Statistics from the National Center for Victims of Crime, as reported on its Web site, show that 896,000 children in this country were maltreated in 2004—either by neglect or abuse. Eighty-seven percent of those kids were abused by one or both of their parents.[1]

Teens from abusive households may have been dealing with abuse for years. While they may have adapted to it or found ways to cope with it, they will always bear its scars. Many of the coping mechanisms they develop are negative ones.

Major Carol Cummings of Washington State's King County sheriff's office, in an article entitled "For Children, Neglect Can Hurt as Much as Abuse," points out that children who have been maltreated in any way, including severe neglect, grow up seeing themselves as victims. These kids may go on to victimize others. Children who have been abused, especially by neglect, have a higher incidence of developing criminal behavior patterns.[2]

If you have been abused or have observed a sibling or friend being abused, tell a responsible adult. Talking to someone takes a great deal of courage, but it can be the only way to stop the abuse.

Parent/Teen Conflicts

In his article "Parents and Teens: The Age Old Battle Explored," Dr. Michael S. Tobin expresses his dismay that we continue to have the same types of conflicts between parents and teens generation after generation. He does believe, however, that some of these conflicts are healthy. Many of these conflicts occur because teens are pushing for more freedom, one of the first steps in the long march to maturity. Conflicts arise when teens want more freedom than their parents feel they can handle. In an effort to protect kids from mistakes they them-selves may have made when they were teens, parents sometimes impose strict rules with which they expect their kids to comply. Teens frequently ignore the rules or actively rebel against them.[3]

Conversely, teens can also be stressed if their parents are not involved enough in their lives. An anonymous teen correspondent published an article on this issue, entitled "On Teen Stress: Pressure, Loneliness and Discontentment" for Wholefamily.com. The writer suggests that parents either forget or ignore the fact that being there for their kids is extremely important.[4]

Teens belonging to the organization Students Against Destructive Decisions (SADD) published an article called "Teens Report Parental Inattention to Their Important 'Rites of Passage' Has High Price Tag." This article also suggests that lack of parental involvement is very stressful to teens. According to SADD, almost half of American high school teens say their parents do not pay attention to important events in their lives. Birthdays, school changes, the onset of puberty, receiving a driver's license, graduating from high school, and starting to date are all events that teens felt were important transitions in their lives. SADD says teens whose parents ignored these events are twice as likely to report daily stress and twice as likely to report being bored or depressed. They are also much more likely to engage in high-risk behaviors, like drinking, drug use, and dangerous driving.[5]

Too much or too little interaction between parents and teens can lead to lots of stress. If you find yourself in either of these situations, you have a big challenge ahead of you. By making a concerted effort to open lines of communication with your folks, a coping mechanism that will be discussed later, you have a good chance of greatly reducing family conflict and the stress it brings.

Divorce

Divorce leaves long-lasting scars on all of those involved. One of the most significant teen stressors created by divorce is the guilt that teens feel when their parents separate and divorce. Moreover, the stress of divorce has been shown to have effects later in life. In "Stark Legacy of Pain for Kids of Divorce," written by Elizabeth Fernandez for Divorcesource.com, data from a study cowritten by Judith Wallerstein and Julia Lewis were reviewed. In that study, children from sixty middle-class families in which parents divorced were followed for twenty-five years to see what long-term effects the stress of divorce had on them. At the time of the divorce, the study reports that young kids felt fears of abandonment and starvation. When these kids became teens, half became seriously involved with drugs and alcohol. Many of them became sexually active in early adolescence. One of the long-term effects that became apparent when these kids reached adulthood was that they were extremely anxious about their own marriages. Fifty-seven percent of them were single at the time of this report because they remembered the depression and sadness created by their parents' divorces.[6]

Perhaps your parents divorced when you were younger, or you are facing this extremely stressful situation now. Talking with an adult who is not directly involved—a school counselor, a teacher, or even the parent of a friend—may help you get through this difficult time.

Illness and Death

A major illness or the death of a parent or sibling is extremely stressful for a teen. Dealing with grief, wanting to be supportive for the remaining parent or both parents, and still coping with all the other stresses of teen life can be overwhelming. Teens feel that they should be the supporters when all they really want to do is be supported. In a discussion of the effects of grief and loss on teens, staff members from the psychiatry department at Cincinnati Children's Hospital Medical Center say:

> Normally, children and teens may experience a temporary difficulty in functioning at school or in social situations [after a loss] . . . but there is no time limit for grieving. It may take years for some people to resolve, accept, or forgive the loss.[7]

Chronic Illness

The stress that having a chronic illness places on a teen is incalculable. Fortunately, most teens are perfectly healthy and only have to deal with short-term illnesses. Occasionally, though, teens do develop chronic health problems. The initial reaction you may experience when finding out you have a significant health problem with which you will have to cope for the rest of your life is total disbelief. The next reaction you will likely experience is anger. Eventually, the reality of this very stressful situation will sink in.

Many chronically ill teens become very depressed and decide that death is preferable to the treatment for their diseases. They disregard or actively rebel against treatment regimens recommended by their physicians. Psychiatrists at Cincinnati Children's Hospital, recognizing the tremendous stress chronically ill teens experience, confirm that being stressed out negatively affects the ability to make rational decisions.[8] When your health is the issue, you need all the information and help you can get to decide on your best course of action. Don't be too rebellious to seek out help.

SCHOOL ISSUES

American kids spend a majority of their time in school, where they learn, make friends, and start developing their value systems. They are subjected to many significant stressors. Although each of you has your own unique set of stressors, surveys of several groups of your peers have identified five categories of school-related stressors that they feel are paramount.

Living up to parental expectations about their performance in school is extremely stressful for many teens. This is especially true if they feel their parents' expectations are unrealistic, or if teens feel the need to be as good as or better than an older sibling.[9] Most parents want their children to succeed, and school performance is one parameter that a parent looks at to judge whether a child is on the right track. What a parent considers to be the "right track," however, and what a teen thinks it is can be quite different.

What do you do if your parents think you should pursue courses strong in the sciences, but your real interests and talents are in the arts? Conflicts like these are major stressors. They become even more significant if you can't talk to your parents about the problem or are unable to find a compromise that all of you can live with. It would be helpful to talk with a teacher or school counselor who could give you advice about the best way to deal with such conflicts.

Grades

Getting good grades was one of the top-five, greatest school stressors listed by teens in several surveys. Ideally, all of us would study and strive for good grades just for the love of learning. In reality, the push for good grades is often driven by things other than the love of learning. In order to participate in most sports programs and to be recruited to play college sports, students must maintain a high grade point average. In an article entitled "What Type of Skills Do College Coaches Look For in Recruits?," its author, Justin Graves, reports on an interview with former Alabama State College's softball coach Larry Keenam. Coach Keenam said, "After effort, the player must be coachable, intelligent, have class, and be an athlete. The most important thing is that they are able to make the grades. If they can't, they are useless to us."[10]

Being accepted to a prestigious university is very important to some teens. They believe a degree from a famous school will help them get a high-paying job when they graduate. In 2002, economists Alan Krueger and Stacy Dale designed a study to see if this hypothesis was true. In reporting the results of their study, Krueger said, "The average graduate from a top school is making nearly a hundred and twenty thousand dollars a year; the average graduate from a moderately selective school is making ninety thousand dollars." He does go on to say, however, that the difference may reflect the motivation of the kids rather than differences in the schools.[11]

Teens also believe that being admitted to top schools depends on getting very high grades. Again, they are correct. An article on college admissions in the United States says, "Among the most important factors in college admissions are high school grades, difficulty of a student's high school course selection, and scores on the SAT or ACT exams."[12] Applications to American universities and colleges jumped 27 percent between

1985 and 1996. In 2000, Wylie Mitchell, the dean of admissions of Bates College in Lewiston, Maine, said, "The competition, the number of kids applying, has doubled in the last twenty years and that's putting some real pressures on these students."[13]

Activity Overload

Activity overload is another source of stress for teens. A teen quoted in the article "The Frenzy of the Fast Lane" said, "I get upset a lot because there's just so much going on. It's like, 'Oh my God, when is this going to end?'"[14] High school counselors will probably tell you that it takes more than grades for a teen to get into a good college or university. But how much more? College admission committees look at students' extracurricular activities. Have they successfully held down jobs, done volunteer work, showed leadership skills in organizations, or developed athletic, artistic, or musical skills? This criteria gives admission committee members a feel for what a student's interests are. Teens may be carrying the push to be "well-rounded" too far, however. Many are packing so much into their lives that they are truly stressed out.

An article looking at college admission criteria in various countries reports that in the United States, the importance of extracurricular activities in admissions to colleges is overestimated. Having no extracurricular activities to report on an admissions application may be damaging, but reporting an incredible number may not be hugely helpful. Since college admissions officers generally consider it impossible to measure or compare the quality of a student's extracurricular activities, your chances of being admitted to a college is not necessarily enhanced by the number of extracurricular activities you report.[15] Nonetheless, teens are being overwhelmed by the demands on their time. Learning to say "no" diplomatically is difficult, but it is perhaps one of the greatest skills one can learn.

Deciding on Colleges

Making decisions about which college to attend, or whether to go to college at all, is a stressful responsibility for many teens. Should you try for a certain college because "that's where Mom/Dad went"? Should you follow your friends to the local community college? Should you apply to ten colleges or two? All of these questions weigh heavily on teens, even those still in middle school. What if you think you would rather pursue a trade under an apprenticeship or another on-the-job training program? What will your folks think? Will your friends think you are just lazy? Do you care what they think? Of course you care. While bucking parental expectations and peer pressure creates stress, doing what you really want to do may be worthwhile in the long run. If lifestyle and salary are the issues you are considering, you may be pleasantly surprised to find that as a journeyman plumber or an aviation technologist trained in a two- to three-year apprenticeship program, you will have more regular work hours and undoubtedly make a better salary than most of your college-educated peers will over a working lifetime.

Changing Schools

In our relatively mobile society, kids are frequently subjected to the stress of changing schools. Younger teens count this as one their top-five school stressors. Finding a place to fit in and finding new friends are of more concern than academic stressors in this situation. Moving from grade school to middle school, then from middle school to high school, also stresses many kids. Compared to elementary schools, which are relatively nurturing, middle schools can be quite intimidating. An article entitled "Anxiety in Children" on Lifepositive.com reports on work from researchers at the University of Michigan. The researchers showed that, on average, children's grades drop dramatically during the first year of middle school compared with their grades in elementary school. Kids tend to develop what the researchers call "middle school malaise," with loss of interest in academics and increased interest in fitting in with the crowd.[16] The transition to high school can be equally stressful, especially if the high schools into which teens are moving are considerably larger than the middle schools from which they came.

PEER-GROUP PRESSURES

For some teens, having one or two good friends to pal around with is all they need to be comfortable. Others want to fit into a larger group and be accepted and respected by the members of that group. Regardless of how many people make up your peer group, you will find that their opinions are very important. Your peer group, whether large or small, can have an incredible amount of influence on you. Decisions about whether or not to go along with the crowd will have to be made on many occasions. These decisions may be difficult and stressful to make. Let's look at some areas in which you may feel a lot of pressure from your peers.

Dating

Mediamark surveyed 4,600 teens who had a boyfriend or girlfriend. Fifty-three percent said their relationships caused them stress.[17] Causes of stress among dating couples vary. It is not unusual for both members of a couple to be very busy with school, sports, and work. In this instance, they frequently feel that they have to "steal" time to be with each other. In some cases, one partner is busier than the other. The less busy partner feels that he or she is given second place to everything else—a very stressful situation for both members of the couple.

Dating violence was also listed as a major stressor for some teens. Dating violence is defined as the intentional use of abusive tactics and physical force in order to obtain and maintain power and control over an intimate partner.[18] According to the U.S. Department of Health and Human Services, one out of four teens may be in a relationship where abuse occurs. The abuse can range from threats to actual physical force of a sexual nature that is meant to cause pain and injury to the teen, either male or female, who is being abused. Dating violence could be a single episode of date rape in which the person raped did not consent to the sexual encounter. However, the term is more often used to describe the physical abuse that some teens repeatedly endure in the mistaken belief that their partner really loves them and is using physically abusive sex "for their own good." Dating violence may start at an early age. In a survey of eighth- and ninth-grade girls, one in twelve admitted to suffering sexual assault on a date.[19]

Date rape should be reported to a responsible adult, as should any dating violence. This may be hard to do, since victims of such violence often feel responsible for what happened to them. They may feel that they have allowed the violence to happen so it is their own fault, or their abusers may have blamed them. Whatever the reason, they are not responsible for the violence that they have endured. Because victims of date rape or dating violence have much difficulty in taking steps to stop the violence, most communities have established hotlines. These are call centers that are manned 24/7 to provide initial help to those who need it. If you are the victim of dating violence, help is at the end of your phone line or even on the Web.

Bullying

The term "bullying" is used to describe a variety of different behaviors, all of which can be very stressful to the one being bullied. Teasing, name calling, intentionally not inviting someone to a party or other social event, ignoring someone, or gossiping about him/her are all forms of bullying. At its extreme, bullying can also involve physical contact, like hitting, pinching, pushing, slapping, or other forms of assault.

"Bullying Behaviors Among U.S. Youth," an article by Tonja R. Nansel, reports on a survey conducted by the World Health Organization in 1998. Almost 16,000 students in grades six through ten were surveyed. Of that group, 29.9 percent reported moderate or frequent involvement in bullying. Thirteen percent of the group were bullied, 10 percent did the bullying, and a little over 6 percent were both victims and perpetrators. Peak bullying behavior was seen in kids in grades six through eight and was less common among ninth and tenth graders.[20]

In an article called "Facts About Bullying," the Wellesley Center for Women identifies the activity as one of the main stressors for school kids today. The article contains statistics from the National Education Association's (NEA) Youth Risk survey, published in 1995. The NEA survey showed that in 1995, as many as 160,000 students in U.S. schools missed classes each day due to fear of attack or intimidation by peers. A second report from the

NEA, published in 2003, suggests that bullying is still a major problem in American schools. It is continuing to create fear in schools and is having a negative impact on learning.[21]

Since most teens today use the latest communication technologies, a new type of bullying has developed. Bill Belsey says, "Cyberbullying involves the use of information and communication technologies such as e-mail, cell phone and pager text messages, instant messaging, defamatory personal Web sites, and defamatory online personal polling Web sites to support deliberate, repeated, and hostile behavior by an individual or group that is intended to harm others."[22] Belsey is a creator and facilitator of a Web site on cyberbullying. Bills are now pending in Congress to make this form of harassment a criminal offense.

As with dating violence, you need to let someone know if you are being bullied. When bullying occurs in schools, alerting a teacher or counselor would be a positive first step. Hotlines are also available to provide help for those being bullied. Since many who are bullied become bullies, getting help early is important to avoid long-term problems. Belsey recommends the following ways to respond to cyberbullying: don't respond to messages from cyberbullies—that's what they want you to do; inform your parents; inform your Internet service provider (ISP) or cell phone/pager provider; inform your local police; don't delete cyberbullying messages—store them as evidence;

NEVER arrange to meet someone you meet online unless your parents go with you; and set up new e-mail and cell/pager accounts.

Belonging

Wanting to be accepted as a member of a group is a normal wish. Not being accepted by the group, or not knowing whether you will be accepted, is very stressful. Most teens belong to some type of group, which are often made up of kids with similar interests or similar ethnic backgrounds. Teens in these types of groups are free to participate as little or as much as they want and frequently change groups as their interests change.

For some, needing to belong somewhere is so important that they join gangs. Some teens even join gangs to gain protection from others who are harassing or threatening them. Today's gangs are groups of teens and young adults who hang out together and are involved in violent or criminal activities. Youth gangs are often organized and controlled by adult criminal leaders who use members of the gang to do their dirty work. For most teens who actually join gangs, membership is usually brief: one-half to two-thirds of teen gang members leave the gang by the end of their first year.[23] Kids who join gangs are usually doing so to try to escape some of the significant stressors in their lives. Unfortunately, in doing so, they create a new set of problems that may be much more serious than those they wish to escape.

Self-Image

The way you perceive yourself may be closely tied to your peer group. It is not uncommon to want to be as attractive and outgoing as the most popular girl in the school or as macho as the captain of the football team. Teens are blitzed by the media with pictures of women and men who look as though they spend all day in the gym. It is no wonder then that 46 percent of the girls and 13 percent of the boys who responded to the MRI Teenmark survey listed weight and body image among their greatest stressors.[24]

Learning to live "in your own skin" is very hard to do, especially if you feel that your appearance is keeping you from being accepted by your peers. Fad diets, different cosmetics, trendy clothes, tattoos, and body piercings are different ways that teens try to improve their self-image.

If you are serious about changing your body image, consulting a dietician and a fitness counselor might be very helpful. There are many professionals available to help you work through self-image issues. How to get in touch with them will be covered in a later chapter of this book.

NATIONAL AND WORLD ISSUES AS STRESSORS

Although it may seem, especially to parents, that teens live in their own little worlds, nothing could be further from the truth. Richard Morin, in "What

Teens Really Think," says, "[Teens] view the future through cracked rose-colored glasses, anxious about the direction of the country and the world. Most predict another terrorist attack as big or bigger than September 11 sometime in their lives. One in four expects a nuclear war."[25]

Morin based his article on a poll of teens in the Washington, D.C., area conducted by the *Washington Post*, Harvard University, and the Henry J. Kaiser Family Foundation. The majority of teens from that survey predicted that pollution, AIDS, drug abuse, immorality, and divorce rates would worsen by the time they were middle-aged. Most expect finding a job, raising a family, or buying a house to be harder than it was for their parents.

National and world issues are especially potent stressors because most teens feel there is nothing they can do about them. Not so! There is plenty you can do right now. Becoming active in groups working to improve and protect the environment and natural resources is becoming increasingly popular with teens. If nature and the environment are concerns for you, check out organizations such as the Sierra Club and the Nature Conservancy, which have many programs for teens and actively encourage youth participation. Political parties can use willing workers, as can groups working to heal differences between cultures and promote world peace. You are also in a position to directly affect national and world events in the future.

VIOLENCE

Escaping violence in our society is almost impossible. The stress of violence is very real for many teens. The National Center for Victims of Crime reported that in 2002, close to 1.7 million teens (ages twelve to nineteen) were victims of violent crime. Of those, more than 1.4 million were physically assaulted, 124,000 were raped or otherwise sexually assaulted, and nearly 115,000 were robbed.[26]

In some respects, our bodies deal with the stress of exposure to violence automatically. As Dr. Selye pointed out many years ago, when we are repeatedly exposed to a stressor, in this case exposure to violence, our bodies adapt so that our "alarm" responses are damped. In other words, we get so used to seeing acts of violence that we no longer react to them with such horror. If you are personally involved in an act of violence, however, you need to get help to deal with the stress—it won't just go away. Talk with an adult you trust, make a hotline call, or seek out a friend to give you some help—then go to the authorities.

You can't escape stress, so you have to cope. Some teens revert to negative coping mechanisms to get through the day, while others harness their stress and use it productively. The next chapters will elaborate on coping mechanisms and will help you to choose healthy ways to deal with your stressors.

CHAPTER SIX

Avoiding Negative Coping Mechanisms

THE QUESTION OF WHETHER OR NOT TO BECOME SEXUALLY ACTIVE AND WHEN IS AN ISSUE FACED BY MOST TEENS.

Y ou have learned to cope with stress in positive ways for most of the time. Occasionally, however, the amount of stress that you face can seem overwhelming. You may try to escape the feeling of being overwhelmed by using negative coping mechanisms, which will eventually create more problems and stress than you had before. Let's look at some of these self-destructive coping mechanisms and why they cannot solve your problems.

ADDICTIVE COPING MECHANISMS

Addiction is a condition in which your life is being controlled by some habit. "Craving," "enslavement," and "dependence" are other words commonly associated with the term "addiction." Smoking, drinking, drug use, and gambling are examples of habits or behaviors that teens use to try to cope with the stressors in their lives. All of them can, and frequently do, become addictions.

Smoking

Tobacco use is an addiction, and nicotine is an addictive drug. According to Dr. John Holbrook, author of "Nicotine Addiction" in *Harrison's Principles of Internal Medicine*, the development of addiction to tobacco is a complex, learned process that involves actual physical changes in the bodies of persons as they experiment with tobacco use.[1] The habit becomes integrated into a smoker's daily activities and, in some instances, may actually control those activities. For example, now that it is illegal to smoke on airplanes, heavy smokers think twice about taking nonstop flights that last longer than three to four hours. For many teens, smoking is a way of dealing with their stressful worlds. In the long run, however, it will only make things worse.

An article, "Smoking," that appeared in the Teen Health section of KidsHealth.org in 2004, says that nine out of ten tobacco users start before they are eighteen years old. One-third of all smokers had their first cigarette before they were fourteen years old.[2] Teens give many reasons for starting to smoke, and several pertain directly to dealing with stress. The most common reason given for starting to smoke was that all of their friends smoked—a good example of the effects of peer pressure. Teens also start to smoke because they believe smoking helps them to relax. Others said they started to smoke as an act of rebellion, and others cited weight loss as a reason for smoking. Statistics show that 6,000 kids a day smoke their first cigarettes. Three thousand kids become daily smokers each day.

While most kids are aware that smoking can lead to major health problems, few of them are farsighted enough to realize that those health problems will be their health problems if they keep smoking. The American Lung Association estimates that if current smoking rates among teens continue, 6.4 million of those teens will die prematurely from a smoking-related disease.[3]

Although nicotine is a very dangerous drug and is extremely addictive, its drug effect has been described as "mild." It doesn't take long for the body of a smoker to adapt to the drug, so smokers need to smoke more and more to get the same buzz they originally got with just a few cigarettes. Nicotine is frequently called a gateway drug because its use frequently leads to the later abuse of alcohol and/or illicit drugs. In 2005, the American Lung Association reported in its "Smoking and Teens Fact Sheet" that teens who smoke are three times more likely to use alcohol, eight times more likely to smoke marijuana, and twenty-two times more likely to use cocaine than those who do not smoke.[4]

Alcohol Abuse

David Elkind, professor of child development at Tufts University, says in his book *All Grown Up and No Place to Go: Teenagers in Crisis*, "Teenagers today drink for the same reason adults do, namely to relieve stress." He goes on to cite a report from the National Institute on Alcohol Abuse and Alcoholism that says more than 1.3 million teens between twelve and seventeen years old have serious drinking problems.[5]

Elizabeth Armstrong and Christina McCarroll, in "Girls Lead in Teen Alcohol Use" in the *Christian Science Monitor*, agree with Dr. Elkind and elaborate on the reasons for underage alcohol use. They say, "Start with alcohol's huge presence in American culture, add more absent parents and rising rates of stress and depression among youths, and you have a cocktail of reasons explaining underage alcohol use."[6] Both of these published reports implicate stress as a major reason for teenage drinking. Peer pressure, a desire to appear sophisticated because the media presents drinking as sexy and cool, and rebellion all contribute to teenage drinking.

Does drinking alcohol really relieve stress? When an alcoholic beverage is consumed, most of the ethanol in that beverage is absorbed into the blood in the first part of the small intestine. Therefore, alcohol gets into the bloodstream in a hurry. It takes about thirty minutes before the full effects of the drink are felt, but the brain gets its first jolt within thirty seconds. Most drinkers think that alcohol does relieve stress because they initially feel good after taking a drink. They think that alcohol is a stimulant, but it is a depressant.

Alcohol is eliminated from the body much more slowly than it is absorbed. It takes men about one hour to eliminate or metabolize the alcohol from one drink, while it takes women slightly longer. If you spend a full hour drinking a beer or sipping a class of wine, you may never experience its depressant effects because the alcohol is being eliminated about as rapidly as it is being consumed. Few drinkers do that though. Most have at least two drinks within an hour, and although they may not realize it, they are already impaired. It takes only three to four drinks within an hour for a man to be legally drunk, while a woman might be legally drunk with only two drinks in an hour. A blood alcohol content of 0.08 percent is considered legally drunk in all U.S. states.

In two weeks of drinking a couple of beers a day, your body adapts to the alcohol. Then you have to increase your alcohol consumption considerably to get the high that you used to get with just two drinks. Your brain cells adapt to having alcohol in the system. Once that happens, you are addicted and may experience withdrawal symptoms if you stop drinking. These symptoms can range from mild hand tremors, stomach upset, and excessive sweating to potentially life-threatening confusion, severe depression, hallucinations, and even seizures.[7]

Like all of the addictive coping mechanisms, drinking alcohol does not relieve stress—it adds to your stress level.

Drug Abuse

In 1994, 45.6 percent of high school seniors reported using illicit substances. The percentage rose to 53 percent by 2002. The Wanatchee, Washington, chapter of SADD has compiled statistics on six of the most commonly used illegal substances in the United States. In 2002, the most commonly used drug for all teens was marijuana. Nineteen percent of younger teens (eighth graders) reported using it, while the number of teens in the twelfth grade who had tried marijuana rose to almost 49 percent. Fewer than 10 percent of teens of any age had tried cocaine, and fewer than 5 percent used heroin. Tranquilizers, methamphetamines, and ecstasy were reportedly used by 5 to 11 percent of the students.[8]

Boredom and high stress were the two main rationalizations for drug use mentioned in a report published August 19, 2003, on CBSNews.com. The report cited a survey conducted by Columbia University that involved 1,987 teens between the ages of twelve and seventeen. Students who characterized themselves as being "frequently bored" were 50 percent more likely than those who were not bored to smoke, drink, and use illegal drugs. Kids suffering from stress were noted to be twice as likely as those with low stress to use illegal drugs. This study, like others, suggested that girls were more stressed than boys. The main stressors identified by this group were academic worries and pressures to have sex and take drugs.[9]

Drug abuse is one step in a series of events in addictive behavior. Dr. Charles Irwin and Dr. Mary-Ann Shafer say in their article "Adolescent Health Problems" that kids who start smoking early are likely to try alcohol and eventually graduate to using marijuana and other illicit drugs.[10] They find they need more potent drugs in ever-increasing quantities to get relief from their stressors. At some point, the stressors that caused teens to seek drugs in the first place become secondary to cravings for the drugs themselves. These teens are truly self-destructing.

Gambling

Youth gambling is a fairly recent phenomenon. Most kids gamble for fun—and many of the gambling activities in which they are involved are actually innocent games played at parties. Dr. Jeff Derevensky, a professor of child psychology and a psychiatrist at McGill University in Montreal, Canada, says that 80 percent of kids gamble at least once a year. Most of them do this for fun and recreation, but as many as 4 to 8 percent of them develop gambling problems. More than one million teens between the ages of twelve and eighteen are compulsive gamblers.[11]

According to Elizabeth George, executive director of the North American Training Institute, many teens start gambling to escape the stress of parental conflicts or the stress of broken relationships. Once they start, they get hooked—and many become compulsive gamblers.[12] Many stressed teens are significantly depressed and have very low self-esteem. When these teens gamble and win, they get a boost in self-esteem. They find this boost gratifying. Unfortunately, they can get hooked on gambling, start to lose, and become more depressed and stressed.[13]

Casual Sex

The question of whether or not to become sexually active and when is an issue faced by most teens. Family values, religious beliefs, peer-group pressure, and personal values all play a part in a teen's decision. For many teens, there may be conflicts between what they have been brought up to believe about sexual relationships and what they are being encouraged to do by potential sexual partners. This can create a tremendous amount of stress. Teens who are consciously making a decision about becoming sexually active are probably doing so with a single sexual partner in mind. It is likely that both partners will insist on the use of condoms or another contraceptive. These are not kids participating in casual, or promiscuous, sex.

At the other extreme are teens who are frequently under a lot of pressure by their peers to "get with the program," which all too often includes having sexual relations with several partners. Promiscuous sex, like drinking and drug use, becomes another way of fitting into the group. In 2003, the Centers for Disease Control and Prevention reported that 47 percent of high school students said they were sexually active. Fourteen percent of those said they have had more than four sexual partners. Alarmingly, 37 percent did not use condoms during intercourse.[14] Having multiple sexual partners and failing to use condoms are characteristics of promiscuity.

There is a very strong association between promiscuity and the addictive mechanisms used by many teens to cope with stress. Katie Dillard, in a publication for Advocates for Youth called "Adolescent Sexual Behavior II: Socio-Psychological Factors," says that smoking, an addictive coping mechanism, is the best predictor of sexual activity in sixth graders. The use of alcohol is strongly associated with having intercourse with many partners.

She goes on to say, "Seventeen percent of teens, ages 13 to 18, who have had sex say that they had intercourse under the influence of drugs or alcohol when they might not have otherwise done so."[15]

Dillard also reports that there is a high correlation between having casual sex and having been sexually abused, one of the greatest stressors a teen can face. A survey of 4,000 high school teens showed that 30.2 percent of girls and 9.3 percent of boys participating in the survey had been sexually abused. The abused teens were more likely than those who were not abused to report multiple sexual partners, using drugs during sexual encounters, and becoming pregnant.

Like addictive coping mechanisms, promiscuity can lead to many more problems than it solves. The United States has the highest teen pregnancy rate of all developed countries. About one million teens become pregnant each year. Eighty percent of those pregnancies are unintended, and 50 percent end in abortion.[16] In addition to pregnancy, sexually transmitted diseases are potential problems for those practicing casual sex. Ten American teens are diagnosed with AIDS each day. More than 20,000 young people between thirteen and twenty-four years old become HIV infected each year. There are about nineteen million new STD cases reported each year in the United States. One-half of these are in teens fifteen through nineteen years of age.[17] These facts reinforce the premise that destructive coping mechanisms create many more stressors than they relieve.

THE COMPANY YOU KEEP

Gangs are a source of stress for many teens and, conversely, are frequently sought by teens looking for ways to escape stress. The Web site Gangs and At-Risk Kids lists reasons that teens join gangs. Among them are several that are directly related to coping with stress. Many teens want be members of a group in which they will be respected. Not finding this group among their school acquaintances can lead them to join a gang that they think will offer them friendship. Some teens join to conform with kids in their neighborhood or ethnic group. Others join because they are being hassled, bullied, or abused. They think that by joining a gang they will be protected from their bullies or abusers.[18]

Stressors at home can make kids turn to gangs. The gang members become their new family, forging a very strong bond. These teens are most likely to come from homes where they have been physically and emotionally abused. They join gangs to get away from what they perceive to be excessive parental control. By doing so, they place themselves in the position of being used by the adults who organize and direct gangs. Gang members are usually controlled by alcohol and drugs, and they do all the work, take all the risks, and are totally expendable.

Teen gang members are much more likely than other teens to commit serious and violent crimes. In Denver, Colorado, for instance, 14 percent of teens are gang members. These kids were responsible for 89 percent of violent crimes in Denver in 1997. Gang members are at least sixty times more likely to be killed than non-gang members.[19]

ERNESTO'S STORY

Ernesto was having trouble remembering how it felt not to be scared. He truly knew what being the "runt of the litter" meant. He was the youngest of three boys and had always been small for his age. He was frequently the object of his brothers' bullying, as they were of their father's. Even at school, he was often the brunt of others' cruelty.

That had been two years before Ernesto's introduction to Los Vatos, "the Comrades." At first, Ernesto thought a miracle had happened. He suddenly had new friends who thought he was worth protecting. His older gang "brothers" were what he had always dreamed his real brothers would be like—they teased but didn't bully, expected him to help but didn't demand, and always seemed to be interested in his ideas.

Then things changed. Los Vatos had a new leader who made no bones about the fact that members did what they were told or they were gone. Ernesto had been told to do a lot of things in the last few weeks that were more than scary—they were terrifying. He did them because he was too scared not to. "Being gone" had permanent implications. Now here he was, sitting in the back of the 42nd Street bus on the way to make a delivery to a pusher who operated near his old school—he was still small enough and looked young enough to pass for one of the students. How many kids would he screw up if he did this job? Was belonging to a gang important enough to play with other people's lives? How had he gotten into this mess? Could he get out of it?

Ernesto, who frequently rode the 42nd Street bus, had read every advertisement on its walls a thousand times before. One of them suddenly jumped out at him. "Need Help?" one sign asked. "We're Here for You! Just Call the National Youth Crisis Hotline."

Could he do it? Just as the bus pulled to a stop in front of Tilly School, he pulled his cell phone out of his pocket. Did he have the guts to do it? He thought so.

SUICIDE

Suicide is the third leading cause of death among adolescents and young adults fifteen to twenty-four years of age. In 2001, 1,611 teens fifteen to nineteen years of age and 272 kids between the ages of ten and fourteen committed suicide in the United States.[20]

Most teens who attempt suicide do so to escape from extremely stressful situations that seem impossible to deal with in any other way. More than half of teen suicides occur in depressed kids. Mild depression occurs in up to 10 percent of high school students; 1 to 2 percent have major depression.

Teens who have had a family member or a close friend commit suicide are more likely to attempt suicide. A recent death in the family is another predisposing factor. Substance abuse is also associated with suicides and suicide attempts. Alcohol and some drugs have depressive effects on the brain. Teens who are stressed and depressed may turn to alcohol and drugs to escape their symptoms, only to find that they are even more depressed. Alcohol and drugs impair a person's ability to assess risks, make good choices, and think of solutions to problems.[21]

Not all suicides are planned. A suicide attempt is a call for help. Many teens have trouble telling their parents and friends how they feel. They look at attempting suicide as a way of letting these people know that they are hurting. Unfortunately, what starts out as an attempt may end in the death of the teen—a terrible solution to a temporary problem.

If you are experiencing significant depression and think there are no solutions to your problems, talk to someone about how you feel before your depression deepens to the point that you are unable to ask for help. If you feel that you can't talk with your parents, remember that there are hotlines available in almost every community in the country, and there are also national toll-free numbers that you can call to get help. The key is to talk to someone.

CHAPTER SEVEN

Take Control

BEING ABLE TO LET OTHERS KNOW WHAT YOU THINK AND FEEL IS IMPORTANT.

David Elkind, in *All Grown Up and No Place to Go*, says that each of us has a finite amount of energy to devote to life's activities. If we have to expend a lot of our energy dealing with stressors, we have a lot less to expend on activities that lead to a satisfying life.[1] The trick is to find positive ways to respond to stress—those that will expend the least energy—so that you have plenty left to build a great life.

YOU'VE GOT TO LIKE YOURSELF!

Self-image is the way you see yourself in relation to others. Are you satisfied with your physical appearance or your weight? How's your personality? Do you like yourself and think others like you, too? Improving your self-image is the first step in having a positive "sense of self."

The next step is to develop a healthy self-esteem. Self-esteem is the opinion you have of yourself based on your attitude about many factors in your life. These include your value as a person, your achievements, your purpose in life, your strengths and weaknesses, and your independence.

STEPS TO A BETTER SENSE OF SELF

So how do you improve your self-image and boost your self-esteem? The first step to improving self-image is to list things you like about yourself. As you do that, you will undoubtedly think of things you do not like about yourself. It is very important, however, to question whether your view of those things is accurate, or whether you are being too hard on yourself. For instance, you may think of yourself as overweight or underweight, not because you are but because you are comparing yourself to popular images of people on TV or in magazines. If, realistically, changes need to be made to improve your self-image, start with easy ones such as changing your hairstyle, beginning an exercise program, or getting a few new clothes. Take a positive approach to things that are harder to change, like your weight. Think of them as challenges instead of obstacles.[2]

As you improve your self-image, you will find that you are also strengthening your self-esteem. Here are a few other suggestions to help you improve self-esteem.

Use Positive Speech

If you stop to think about it, you are constantly having mental conversations with yourself. If you bad-mouth yourself in these conversations, you may soon believe you are a bad person. Put a positive spin on your mental conversations rather than a negative one. For instance, if you have done badly on a test at school, instead of saying to yourself, "You dummy, how could you be so stupid?" think, "Wow, that was a hard test. I really need to study harder for the next one."

Be tolerant of your own mistakes. Nobody is perfect. It is easy to be excessively critical of yourself, especially when things are not going well. Mistakes happen, but the key is to admit when you make one, learn from it, then let it go.

Acknowledge Your Accomplishments

Most teens feel that passing the test to get their driver's license is a big accomplishment. You should also recognize your smaller accomplishments each day. Make a list of those things—even if they don't seem very important. By recognizing your accomplishments, you begin to understand that you have self-worth. Be proud of every new day's accomplishments.

Be Assertive

Being able to let others know what you think and feel is important. After all, what you have to say is just as important as what others have to say. As a teen, you may think that your parents or other adults do not want to know what you think or what is important to you. Most adults welcome conversations with teens. Having a give-and-take conversation with kids is one of the joys of parenthood. So say what you think, but also listen to others and respect their opinions.

Spend time with people who value you. Listen to what they say about you. People you choose to be around are often mirrors of how you feel about yourself. If others are constantly putting you down, you're running with the wrong crowd!

TAKING CONTROL

With your self-image buffed and your self-esteem maximized, you are ready to deal with stress and make it work for you. Here are a few steps that will help you to take control.

Define the Problem

Know that you cannot eliminate all stress from your life. Who can? Define your individual list of major stressors. Take the time to analyze your day. Actually write down how you spent your time, with whom you interacted, and how you responded to situations and events.

It is especially important to note your feelings—were you happy, sad, or infuriated? Keep track of these things for several days, then set aside an hour or so to analyze your notes. You may be surprised to find out what did or did not cause you stress. Once you know what your major stressors are, you can formulate a plan to deal with them.

Learn to Manage Your Time

One of the main stressors identified by teens is the lack of time to do everything that is expected of them. Part of this problem may center on inefficient use of time. Do you interrupt your homework to chat on the phone and find that two hours later your book report is still not finished?

Do you sit down to read a chapter of your history book, but end up reading the evening paper instead? These "time stealers"[3] are just examples of ways you may be using your time inefficiently. Good time management enables you to schedule activities you have to do, as well as those you want to do.

List those daily and weekly activities that you know you have to do. For instance, if there is a science fair project due on Friday, list the fair and the times during the week that you are setting aside to work on the project. Always list your routine commitments, like classes, band practice, student council meetings, or after-school jobs. After you get all of the "must-dos" into your schedule, start filling in uncommitted time slots with things you should do, like getting a head start on research for a term paper or volunteering to help with your kid brother's school carnival. You are in control of this schedule, so build time into it for everything: "alone" time, family time, recreational time, or even time to sleep. Keep this schedule with you so you can update it during the day and week.

Realistically, no schedule will ever be perfect. Your friends will still call to chat or want you to go out at inopportune times, and occasionally you will rebel against the regimentation you are imposing on yourself. If you stick with it most of the time, though, you will find even an incredibly busy schedule to be much less stressful than it was before. You are in control.

Learn to Say No

Sally Byrne in "Coping with Stress" suggests keeping a schedule as mentioned above, but seriously consider your motives for scheduling certain activities.[4] For instance, are you working twenty hours a week to save money for college tuition, or to buy your tenth pair of Nikes? Maybe fewer Nikes and more time would be helpful to you. She also suggests that you may agree to do a lot of things you don't want to do simply because you think you should. To some extent that is unavoidable. For instance, your mother may have suggested that you volunteer to help with your brother's school carnival. You don't really want to do it, but it is important to your mother and your brother, and they are important to you—so you do it. On the other hand, you don't have to say yes when asked to be on a committee to plan an activity in which you have no interest. Guard your time—no one else will.

Practice and Prepare

One of the most stressful things you can do is to approach an event without preparation. For example, perhaps one of the requirements for your history class is that you give a brief talk on a historical subject of your choice. You've chosen to discuss Lewis and Clark and their "Voyage of Discovery." You know the material cold, but the thought of presenting it puts you in a panic.

Practice your talk in front of a mirror beforehand. Give the talk to your parents, a friend, or even your dog. You will find that because you have practiced and are prepared, you have harnessed your stress and made it work for you. When the time comes to present your subject, you will be more relaxed than if you had not prepared.

Finish What You Start

With your busy schedule, you may find that you never quite finish anything to your satisfaction. Projects or chores that you started weeks ago are still hanging over your head while you try to deal with more urgent matters. Eventually, everything piles up and you may begin to feel overwhelmed. You can minimize stress by making a concerted effort to finish each project or chore as it comes along. Break big chores into a group of smaller tasks that can be completed in a reasonable amount of time. Soon, the entire project will be done. You will get a great deal of satisfaction from actually finishing something you've started.

Be Good to Your Body

Coping with outside stressors if you are physically stressed is very difficult. The "big three" of staying physically healthy are to eat right, get enough sleep, and get plenty of exercise.

Stress reactions require your body to expend tremendous amounts of energy. Where do you get the fuel for these reactions? From food, of course. Eating on the run, as you do when you are particularly busy, probably means you are eating a lot of fast food, snacks, and sodas. These foods are high in calories, fats, and caffeine and low in basic nutrients, vitamins, and minerals. Not only is your body not getting what it needs to help you fuel your stress reactions, it is being overwhelmed with things that may worsen these reactions. So take the time to eat well-rounded meals.

Your body also needs water to keep all your systems working. Very few teens take the time to drink enough water, and most are usually dehydrated. Some symptoms of dehydration are similar to those of depression. You may feel tired, cranky, or weepy, and can experience nausea and faintness. Simply drinking water can make all of these symptoms disappear.

Sleep deprivation problems can add to the stressors in your life. The question is, why do we need to sleep? Most people need between seven and eight hours of sleep a night. Most teens, however, don't get that much. Melatonin, a hormone that regulates sleeping and waking patterns, is produced later at night in teens than it is in younger kids and in adults. Teens tend to fall asleep later at night and, if their schedules allow, sleep later in the morning. Teens who fall asleep after midnight may still have to be up early for school, so over time they may become sleep deprived. Sleep deprivation leads to impairment in judgment and the ability to think, and may also lead to impairment of motor skills and reaction times. This can have serious consequences, especially if sleep-deprived teens are driving.[5]

The third essential in taking care of your body is to get plenty of exercise. Exercise has three major benefits in helping to control stress. First, it helps to counterbalance the added caloric intake that is common in kids on the run. By expending some of those extra calories in physical activity, teens are less likely to put on the pounds and have an easier time maintaining positive self-images. Exercise can decrease stress by causing increased production of endorphins, natural opioids, in the brain. This gives a natural high that counterbalances the lows of stress. The third benefit of exercise is that you get an outlet for all the pent-up energy that stress produces. By expending this energy productively, you are less likely to react impulsively and violently in situations.

CHAPTER EIGHT

Help

OTHERS CAN BE THERE FOR YOU IF YOU ASK.

Y ou are surrounded by stressors. Most of the time you have little trouble handling these problems. There are times, however, when you simply may not be able to go it alone. Earl Hipp, clinical psychologist and author of *Fighting Invisible Tigers: A Stress-Management Guide for Teens*, says that the most challenging thing you have to do in dealing with severe stress is to admit to yourself that you need help.[1] This is not a sign of weakness; it is a sign of a very strong person.

Dr. Donna Widener, a former tutor and stress management counselor at the University of Oregon, says kids often want help but don't know how or whom to ask. She suggests that they ask themselves these three questions before they reach out to someone:

1. Why do I think I need help?
2. How severe are my stressors? Are they day-to-day problems, like trying to manage time or meeting obligations? Are they bigger things such as trying to cope with life transitions or peer pressure? Or are they truly traumatic stressors like being raped or being hooked on drugs?
3. What kind of help do I need?[2]

By clarifying the answers to these questions in your mind, you are more likely to ask the right person for help. You will also be able to express your needs more clearly when you do ask for help.

REACH OUT AND TRUST SOMEONE

Once you have decided that you need help, the challenge is to reach out and trust someone. Whom can you talk to? Who will listen and not be judgmental? Who can help you? Although it may be hard to believe at times, you are not alone. Others can be there for you if you ask. Care and support may be found among friends and family. If you seek an ear outside of your circle, school counselors, therapists, and support groups can be great resources.

Parents

Those of you who can talk easily with your parents are truly lucky. You know that you can take even the most stressful situation to them and be assured of getting sound advice. However, about 40 percent of teens who responded to the surveys discussed earlier indicated that they were stressed by parent/teen conflicts. Almost all of these kids indicated that the inability to communicate with their folks created many of these conflicts. The reasons for these communication problems are varied. Ironically, the very fact that you are maturing may be one of the prime problems.

Dr. Judith Rapaport from the National Institute of Mental Health followed 145 kids from childhood into their teen years with special brain scans (magnetic resonance imaging) to see what happened to their brains as they aged. She found that at about the same time the kids reached puberty, their brain scans showed enlargement of the frontal lobes. This part of the brain is the area where planning, reasoning, and impulse control occur. With various psychological test methods, she found that these kids—most of whom were teens by this point—had improvement in their problem-solving skills, demonstrated the ability to make responsible choices, and were already developing their own beliefs and values. In other words, they were maturing.[3]

"So what?" you ask. How does all this relate to talking or not talking to your parents? In "Talking to Your Parents—or Other Adults," the authors point out that while you are gaining confidence in yourself and your ability to resolve problems, your parents are having a hard time realizing that you aren't the little kid for whom they have been making decisions all these years.[4] The disparity of how you see yourself and how your parents see you can lead to disagreements. In some cases, you may decide that you simply can't talk with you folks and they may decide the same thing. When you run into stressors that you can't handle alone, in spite of your new maturity, it is frequently hard to reopen new lines of communication with your parents. A strategy for talking with your parents about difficult issues was suggested in this same article.

Define the issues you want to discuss with your parents. You may find it helpful to actually write down the most important points you want to cover so you don't forget them. Limit these to three or four main topics. Be clear that you have an important issue you want to discuss. Schedule your talk for a specific time when you will have their undivided attention. Finally, write your thoughts out and give them to your parents before the discussion.

Family and Friends

There may be times when you simply cannot talk with your parents. Fortunately, there are other adults available. A favorite teacher, coach, member of a religious group, grandparent, aunt, or uncle can listen and provide comfort. They will also know when to steer you to a professional who can help.

You may even turn to your friends. What are friends? In February 2005, the Nemours Foundation asked teens what it takes to be a good friend. More than 5,000 teens replied to the query. Among other things, kids said friends were people whose wisdom and judgment they valued. They also said that real friends were those who would tell you what you needed to hear, not what you wanted to hear.[5]

If you are scared, depressed, confused, or desperate to escape from a situation or habit that has gotten out of hand, choose a friend you trust who will be brutally honest with you and talk to that person. This friend may already know a lot about what you are feeling.

Support Groups

One of the most effective ways of dealing with a problem is to meet with other people who are experiencing, or who have experienced, the same problem. Usually these groups, which are called support groups, are started by two or three people who work through problems together. Later, as the group expands, the original members provide guidance to newer members. They may call on psychologists, physicians, or other professionals to give help when needed. However, the main advantage of this type of group lies in knowing that others understand the problems you are having because they all have been there personally. Support groups are as close as the nearest telephone. Many have hotlines that you can call if you feel desperate. They honestly care and can help you deal with a crisis and can continue to provide support as long as you need it.

Counselors and Psychotherapists

School counselors are among those professionals whose job is to help kids cope with problems. They have special training in many areas, so they aren't limited to helping with school issues. Counselors are also knowledgeable about the availability of support groups or therapists to whom they can refer you, should you need it.

Sometimes a teen will have problems so troubling that friends and/or parents feel unable to give the teen adequate help. At that point, the teen may have to see a psychotherapist. A therapist is professionally trained to help with emotional and behavioral problems. It's the goal of a therapist to help teens learn about themselves, discover ways to overcome troubling feelings and behaviors, and develop good coping skills.

The approach a therapist uses depends on a teen's individual needs, but it always includes listening, exchanging information, building trust, and respecting confidentiality. In some instances, a therapist may recommend and prescribe medication to help a teen through a crisis. Few require long-term drug therapy. Once a teen and his or her therapist have developed a workable plan for dealing with stressors, it will be up to the teen to implement the plan with the therapist's help. The coping skills learned will be of life-long benefit.

Other Sources of Help

Experts in stress management have written books and made tapes and DVDs on topics ranging from time management to relaxation techniques and everything in between. Perhaps you would like suggestions about visual imaging, meditation, yoga, or aromatherapy. Many of these books, tapes, and DVDs can be found in your public library.

The Internet also has many Web sites dealing with stress and stress management that you can consult, but do so with caution. When you are experiencing stress overload, you may be particularly vulnerable to exploitation by those who advertise quick fixes for all of your woes. If it sounds too good to be true, it probably is.

Be particularly cautious about trying natural medications or supplements that are advertised to relieve stress. Many of these products contain chemicals in amounts that are potentially toxic. There is no agency regulating the companies that make these products, so their efficacy, potency, and purity may not be known. Ask your doctor or therapist about any type of medication or supplement before taking it. You may save yourself a lot of money, not to mention your life.

CONCLUSION

The teen years are a time of major life crises. You are experiencing many physical changes that can be stressful. You are developing your own beliefs and values. You are faced with the necessity and the challenge of deciding about future educational goals, where to take relationships, and how to respond to endless demands on your time. You are also living in an era of unprecedented technological expansion that is mind-boggling. Is there any wonder that you are stressed? The remarkable thing is that you do handle your stressors as well as you do.

As you have seen, there are many ways to cope with stress. Perhaps some of the positive coping mechanisms presented here will prove helpful to you. Underlying all of these is one recurring theme—you are not alone. Regardless of what your stressors are and how hopeless things may seem, talking with someone will help, so give it a try.

TEN QUESTIONS TO ASK ABOUT STRESS

1. Do most teens know when they are under too much stress? If so, how? What are the symptoms?
2. Could I have an underlying medical condition that adds to my stress symptoms?
3. Could my stress make medical problems which I have worse?
4. Are there any tests to determine my cause(s) of stress?
5. If untreated, could stress cause more serious conditions to occur?
6. Can exercise and adequate sleep really help me manage my stress?
7. What lifestyle changes can I make to decrease stress?
8. What substances should I stay away from if I feel really stressed? Why?
9. Are there videos, books, or other printed litera-ture that contains useful information about my symptoms?
10. Would I benefit from seeing a psychologist or psychiatrist?

bacterium Loosely used generic name for any rod-shaped microscopic organism.

cholesterol A white, fatty, crystalline alcohol that is found in bile, egg yolks, and other foods, and in nerve tissues.

chronic Continuing for a long time or recurring frequently.

confidential Communicated in secret or private; not public knowledge.

data A group of facts or statistics.

defamatory Injurious to someone's reputation.

depression Absence of cheer or hope; emotional dejection.

deprivation The state of being deprived or having something taken away.

endorphins Chemicals produced in the brain that can cause euphoria or other positive feelings.

gambling To play a game for money or other stakes.

glucose A simple sugar that is the main energy source for body reactions. Many glucose molecules are combined and stored in the liver and other tissues as glycogen. When needed, glycogen is broken down into smaller glucose molecules.

hormone A chemical substance produced in one place in the body that is carried through the bloodstream to another part of the body where it causes some type of reaction.

hypothalamus The region of the brain that controls the autonomic nervous system by regulating functions such as sleep cycles, appetite, and body temperatures.

immunity The power that a person acquires to resist or overcome an infection.

intima The innermost cells lining the lumen of a blood vessel.

lumens The cavity of a tubular organ, such as a blood vessel.

magnetic resonance imaging (MRI) An imaging method developed in the 1980s that's well adapted for studying the nervous system. The technique involves the use of magnetic fields rather than radiation to create images.

metabolism The sum of all the physical and chemical processes in the body that provide energy for its function.

physiology The study of the function of the organs and other body parts during life.

platelet A tiny, colorless, disc-shaped structure found in blood that, when disrupted, initiates the clotting of blood.

promiscuity Indiscriminate relationships, especially as applied to sexual activity.

rite A ritual or ceremony.

spin Putting a twist on the interpretation of an event. The word is used in politics to describe the way a particular idea is presented to influence thinking.

syndrome A group of signs and symptoms that occur together and characterize a disease or disorder.

toxic Poisonous.

American Institute of Stress
124 Park Avenue
Yonkers, NY 10703
(914) 963-1200
E-mail: stress125@optonline.net
Web site: http://www.stress.org

The institute is a clearinghouse for information on stress. It has a large library and has reprints available.

Canadian Institute of Stress
Medcan Clinic Office, Suite 1500
150 York Street
Toronto, ON M5H 3S5
Canada
(416) 236-4218
E-mail: earle@direct.com
Web site: http://www.
  stresscanada.org

The institute was founded by Dr. Hans Selye and is involved with research into the causes and treatment of stress. It provides educational programs, as well as individual counseling.

Canadian Mental Health
  Association
2160 Yonge Street, 3rd Floor
Toronto, ON M45 2Z3
Canada
(416) 484-7756

E-mail: cmhanat@interlog.com
Web site: http://www.cmha.ca

This is the oldest voluntary organization in Canada. It is a nationwide organization of volunteers that promotes mental health with advocacy, education, research, and service.

Children of the Night
14530 Sylvan Street
Van Nuys, CA 91411
(818) 808-4474
Hotline: (800) 551-1800
Web site: http://www.childrenofthenight.org

This organization provides help for runaways or other children who are in crisis situations.

National Institute of Mental Health
6001 Executive Boulevard, Room 8184
MSC 9663
Bethesda, MD 208992-9663
(301) 443-4513
(866) 615-6464
E-mail: nimhinfo@nih.gov
Web site: http://www.nimh.nih.gov

The institute is the branch of the National Institutes of Health concerned with mental health. Evaluation and treatment, as well as education and research, are its goals.

National Network for Youth
1319 F Street NW, Suite 401
Washington, DC 20004

(202) 783-7949
E-mail: info@NN4Youth.org
Web site: http://www.nn4youth.org

This advocacy organization provides education, networking, and training to champion the needs of runaway, homeless, and disconnected youth.

National Runaway Switchboard (Adolescent
  Crisis Line)
3089 N. Lincoln Avenue
Chicago, IL 60657
(773) 880-9680
E-mail: info@nrscrisisline.org
Web site: http://www.nrscrisisline.org

This organization is a national communication system listing hotlines and Web sites for runaway and homeless youth. Its goal is to keep America's runaway and at-risk youth safe and off the street.

WEB SITES

Due to the changing nature of Internet links, Rosen Publishing has developed an online list of Web sites related to the subject of this book. This site is updated regularly. Please use this link to access the list:

http://www.rosenlinks.com/ccw/stre

Carlson, Richard. *Don't Sweat the Small Stuff for Teens*. New York, NY: Hyperion, 2000.

Covey, Sean. *The 7 Habits of Highly Effective Teens*. New York, NY: Fireside, 1998.

Friel, John, and Linda Friel. *The Seven Best Things Smart Teens Do*. Deerfield Beach, FL: HCI, 2000.

Loos, Barbara. *The Stress Factor*. New York, NY: The Reader's Digest Association, 1998.

Radcliffe, Rebecca. *About to Burst: Handling Stress and Ending Violence—A Message for Youth*. Minneapolis, MN: EASE, 1999.

Seaward, Brian, and Linda Bartlett. *Hot Stones and Funny Bones: Teens Helping Teens Cope with Stress and Anger*. Deerfield Beach, FL: HCI, 2002.

Sluke, Sara Jane, and Vanessa Torres. *The Complete Idiot's Guide to Dealing with Stress for Teens*. Indianapolis, IN: Alpha Books, 2002.

Wilde, Jerry. *Hot Stuff to Help Kids Chill Out: The Anger Management Book*. Richmond, IN: LGR Publishing, 1997.

Buckaleu, M. W. *Drugs and Stress*. New York, NY: Rosen Publishing, 1993.

Chintz, Barbara, ed. *The Stress Factor*. New York, NY: The Reader's Digest Association, 1998.

Elkind, David. *All Grown Up and No Place to Go: Teenagers in Crisis*. Reading, MA: Addison-Wesley Publishing, 1984.

Goudriaan, Anna, Jaap Oosterlaan, Edwin de Beurs, and Wim Van den Brink. "Pathological Gambling: A Comprehensive Review of Biobehavioral Findings." *Neuroscience and Biobehavioral Reviews*, Vol. 28, 2004, pp. 123–141.

Henderson, Deborah. "Teens Report Parental Inattention to Their Important 'Rites of Passage' Has High Price Tag." SADD. December 16, 2005. Retrieved April 16, 2006 (http://www.sadd.org/teenstoday/rites.htm).

Hipp, Earl. *Fighting Invisible Tigers: A Stress-Management Guide for Teens*. Minneapolis, MN: Free Spirit Publishing, Inc., 1995.

National Institutes of Health. "Stress System Malfunction

Could Lead to Serious, Life-Threatening Disease." NIH Backgrounder. September 9, 2002. Retrieved February 23, 2006 (http://www. nih.gov/news/pr/sept2002/nichd-09.htm).

National Library of Medicine. "Stress and Deprivation." June 3, 2005. Retrieved March 26, 2006 (http://www.nlm.nih.gov/hmd/emotions/ stress.html).

Posen, David. "The Principles of Stress." Retrieved February 22, 2006 (http://www.davidposen. com/pages/pricip/princip6.html).

Radcliff, Rebecca. *About to Burst: Handling Stress and Anxiety—A Message for Youth.* Minneapolis, MN: EASE, 1999.

Science Daily. "Research Reveals Likely Connection Between Early-Life Stress and Teenage Mental Health Problems." November 16, 2005. Retrieved February 24, 2006 (http://www.sciencedaily. com/releases/2005/11/051116174754.htm).

Wein, Harrison. "Stress and Disease: New Perspectives." *Word on Health.* October 2000. Retrieved February 23, 2006 (http://www.nih. gov/news/WordonHealth/oct2000/story01.htm).

Witkin, Georgia. *Kidstress.* New York, NY: Viking Penguin, 1999.

Chapter 1

1. Hans Selye, "The Nature of Stress." ICNR.com. Retrieved February 24, 2006 (http://www.icnr.com/articles/thenatureofstress.html).
2. Edric Lescouflair, "Walter Bradford Cannon: Experimental Physiologist, 1871–1945." *Notable American Unitarians: A Daughter's View*. Retrieved February 24, 2006 (http://www.harvardsquarelibrary.org/unitarians/cannon_walter.html).
3. Walter Cannon, *Bodily Changes in Pain, Hunger, Fear and Rage: An Account of Recent Researches into the Function of Emotional Excitement* (New York, NY: Appleton, 1915).

Chapter 2

1. National Institutes of Health, "Stress System Malfunction Could Lead to Serious Life-Threatening Disease." NIH Backgrounder. September 9, 2002. Retrieved February 23,

2006 (http://www.nih.gov/news/pr/sep2002/
nichd-09.htm).

2. Hans Selye, "The Nature of Stress." ICNR.com.
Retrieved February 24, 2006 (http://www.
icnr.com/articles/thenatureofstress.html).

Chapter 3

1. National Institutes of Health, "Stress System
Malfunction Could Lead to Serious Life-
Threatening Disease." NIH Backgrounder.
September 9, 2002. Retrieved February 23, 2006
(http://www.nih.gov/news/pr/sept2002/
nichd-09.htm).

2. Hans Selye, "The Nature of Stress." ICNR.com.
Retrieved February 24, 2006 (http://www.
icnr.com/articles/thenatureofstress.html).

3. Mark Beers and Robert Berkow, eds., *The
Merck Manual of Diagnosis and Therapy*, 17th
edition (Westpoint, PA: Merck and Co., 1999),
pp. 1629, 1654.

4. Rebecca Moran, "Evaluation and Treatment of
Childhood Obesity." *American Family Physician*.
Retrieved March 28, 2006 (http://www.aafp.org/
afp/990215ap/861.html).

5. Maurice Blackman, "You Ask About . . . Adolescent Depression." *Canadian Journal of CME*. May
1995. Retrieved April 1, 2006 (http://www.
mentalhealth.com/mag1/p51-dp01.html).

6. Harrison Wein, "Stress and Disease: New
Perspectives." National Institutes of Health,

Word on Health. October 2000. Retrieved February 23, 2006 (http://www.nih.gov/news/WordonHealth/oct2000/story01.html).

7. National Institutes of Health.

Chapter 4

1. Jannie Carter, "Teens 2003: Have We Really Been There and Done That?" *MetroNews*. July 15, 2003. Retrieved April 2, 2006 (http://ww.aces.edu/urban/metronews/vol2no4/teens.html).

2. "Teens Want to Enjoy Life and Relationships, Not Climb the Corporate Ladder." November 24, 2004. Retrieved April 2, 2006 (http://www.mediamark.com/MRI/docs/pr_11-23-04_tm2004.htm).

3. "Survey Shows High Level of Teen Stress." International Child and Youth Care Network. October 16, 2002. Retrieved March 4, 2006 (http://www.cyc-net.org/today2002/today021016.html).

4. "Americans Engage in Unhealthy Behaviors to Manage Stress." American Psychological Association. February 23, 2006. Retrieved April 22, 2006 (http://apahelpcenter.mediaroom.com/index.php?s = press_releases&item = 23).

5. Georgia Witkin, *KidStress* (New York, NY: Viking Penguin, 1999), pp. 11–18.

6. "Kid Poll—Children Worry Most About Grades, Looks, and Problems at Home." KidsHealth.org. June 17, 2004. Retrieved February 23, 2006

(http://www.kidshealth.org/breaking_news/poll_worry.html).

7. Brad Pistole, "Teen Survey 2." West Arkansas Church of Christ. June 1998. Retrieved February 23, 2002 (http://www.westarkchurchofchrist.org/youth/teensurv2.htm).

8. "17,000 Teens Speak Out Through Landmark National Survey." Taco Bell Foundation. November 30, 1999. Retrieved February 23, 2003 (http://ww.tacobell.com/ourcompany/press.htm).

9. "Teens Want to Enjoy Life and Relationships, Not Climb the Corporate Ladder."

Chapter 5

1. "Child Maltreatment." National Center for Victims of Crime. 2004. Retrieved April 6, 2006 (http://www.ncvc.org/ncvc/main.aspx?dbName = DocumentViewer& DocumentID = 38709).

2. Carol Cummings, "For Children, Neglect Can Hurt as Much as Abuse." *Seattle Post-Intelligencer*. April 14, 2002. Retrieved April 6, 2006 (http://www.seattlepi.nwsource.com/opinion/66018_cummingsop.shtml).

3. Michael Tobin, "Parents and Teens: The Age Old Battle Explored." WholeFamily.com. Retrieved March 4, 2006 (http://www.wholefamily.com/aboutteensnow/relationships_family/parents_and_family/ptbattle.html).

4. "On Teen Stress: Pressure, Loneliness, and Discontentment." WholeFamily.com. Retrieved March 4, 2006 (http://www.wholefamily. com/aboutteensnow/feelings/stress/teen_ view.html).

5. "Teens Report Parental Inattention to Their Important 'Rites of Passage' Has High Price Tag." SADD. December 16, 2005. Retrieved April 6, 2006 (http://www.sadd.org/ teenstoday/rites.htm).

6. Elizabeth Fernandez, "Stark Legacy of Pain for Kids of Divorce." Divorcesource.com. Retrieved April 13, 2006 (http://www.divorcesource. com/CA/ARTICLES/starky.html).

7. "Grief and Loss Stressors." CincinnatiChildrens.org. Retrieved April 6, 2006 (http://www.cincinnatichildrens.org/svc/ alpha/p/psychiatry/teens/real-life/grief.htm).

8. "Psychological Complications of Chronic Illness in Adolescence." CincinnatiChildrens.org. June 2005. Retrieved April 6, 2006 (http://www. cincinnatichildrens.org/health/info/mental/ diagnose/complication.htm).

9. Brad Pistole, "Teen Survey 2." West Arkansas Church of Christ. June 1998. Retrieved February 23, 2006 (http://www. westarkchurchofchrist.org/youth/ teensurv2.htm).

10. Justin Graves, "What Type of Skills Do College Coaches Look For in Recruits?" News Courier. June 16, 2006. Retrieved June 17, 2006 (http://www.enewscourier.com/

sports/local_story_167203046.html?keywork =
secondarystory).

11. Malcolm Gladwell, "Getting In." *The New
Yorker*. October 3, 2005. Retrieved June 17,
2006 (http://www.newyorker.com/printables/
critics/051010crit_atlarge).

12. "College Admissions." Wikipedia. June 11,
2006. Retrieved June 17, 2006 (http://
www.wikipedia.org/wiki/college_admissions).

13. Barbara Walsh, "The Frenzy in the Fast Lane."
20 Below. December 31, 2000. Retrieved
March 4, 2006 (http://20below.mainetoday.
com/press/verge/Lead5.shtml).

14. Ibid.

15. "College Admissions."

16. "Anxiety in Children." Lifepositive.com.
Retrieved February 22, 2006 (http://www.
lifepositive.com/mind/psychology/stress/
anxiety-in-children.asp).

17. "Teen Girls Stressed Out More Than Boys."
December 9, 2003. Retrieved April 2, 2006
(http://www.mediamark.com/MRI/docs/pr_12
_09_03_Teenmark.htm).

18. "Dating in the Hood." Study Guide. Retrieved
April 8, 2006 (http://www.intermedia-inc.com/
guidePDF/DA04.pdf).

19. "Dating Violence Common Among Teens." U.S.
Department of Health and Human Services.
Retrieved April 8, 2006 (http://family.samhsa.
gov/teach/dating.aspx).

20. Tonja Nansel, "Bullying Behavior Among U.S.
Youth." *JAMA*, Vol. 385, No. 16, April 25, 2001.

Retrieved April 13, 2006 (http://jama.ama-assn. org/cgi/content/abstract/285/16/2094).

21. "Facts About Bullying." Wellesley Center for Women. 2006. Retrieved April 13, 2006 (http:// www.wcwonline.org/bullying/fact.html).

22. Bill Belsey, "Cyberbullying." Cyberbullying.org. Retrieved April 5, 2006 (http://cyberbullying. org/main_frame.html).

23. "Gangs—Facts and Figures." National Criminal Justice Reference Service. September 21, 2005. Retrieved April 5, 2006 (http://www.ncjrs.gov/ spotlight/gangs/facts.html).

24. "Teen Girls Stressed Out More Than Boys."

25. Richard Morin, "What Teens Really Think." *Washington Post*. October 23, 2005. Retrieved April 2, 2006 (http://www.washingtonpost. com/wp-dgn/content/article/2005/10/18/ AR2005101801698_pf.html).

26. "Teen Victims." National Center for Victims of Crime. 2004. Retrieved April 2, 2006 (http:// www.ncvc.org/ncvc/main.aspx?dbName = "Doc umentViewer&DocumentID + 38721).

Chapter 6

1. John Holbrook, "Nicotine Addiction," *Harrison's Principles of Internal Medicine*, 14th edition, Chapter 389 (New York, NY: McGraw Hill, 1998), p. 2516.

2. "Smoking." Teen Health. 2004. Retrieved April 13, 2006 (http://kidshealth.org/teen/drug_ alcohol/tobacco/smoking.html).

3. "Smoking and Teen Fact Sheet." American Lung Association. November 2004. Retrieved April 13, 2006 (http://www.lungusa.org/site/pp.asp?c = dvLUK9OoE&b = 39871).

4. Ibid.

5. David Elkind, *All Grown Up and No Place to Go: Teenagers in Crisis* (Reading, MA: Addison-Wesley Publishing, Inc., 1984), p. 220.

6. Elizabeth Armstrong and Christina McCarroll, "Girls Lead in Teen Alcohol Use." *Christian Science Monitor*. July 8, 2004. Retrieved April 13, 2006 (http://seattletimes.nwsource.com/html/living/2002004619_girlsdrinking 14.html).

7. Mark Beers and Robert Berkow, eds., *The Merck Manual of Diagnosis and Therapy*, 17th edition (West Point, PA: Merck & Co., 1999), pp. 1581–1586.

8. "Statistics." SADD. 2003. Retrieved April 21, 2006 (http://whs.wsd.wednet.edu/Faculty/Lynch/SADD/statistics.html).

9. "Teen Boredom Breeds Drug Use." CBSNews.com. August 19, 2003. Retrieved April 1, 2006 (http://www.cbsnews.com/stories/2002/09/04/national/printable520718.shtml).

10. Charles Irwin and Mary-Ann Shafer, "Adolescent Health Problems," *Harrison's Principles of Internal Medicine*, 14th edition (New York, NY: McGraw-Hill, 1998), p. 35.

11. Kathy Bunch, "Child's Play." MedicineNet.com. February 12, 2001. Retrieved April 16, 2006 (http://www.medicinenet.com/main/art.asp?articlekey = 51662).

12. Ibid.

13. "Is Your Child a Gambler?" HealthAtoZ.com. June 2005. Retrieved April 16, 2006 (http://www.healthatoz/Atoz/hc/chi/teen/alert04012000_pr.jsp).

14. "Healthy Youth." CDC.gov. Retrieved April 16, 2006 (http://www.cdc.gov/HealthyYouth/sexualbehaviors/index.htm).

15. Katie Dillard, "Adolescent Sexual Behavior II: Socio-Psychological Factors." Advocates for Youth. November 2002. Retrieved April 16, 2006 (http://www.advocatesforyouth.org/publications/factsheet/fsbehsoc.htm).

16. "Teen Pregnancy." National Women's Health Information Center. 1998. As reported in Quick Stats on Female Adolescents. Retrieved April 2, 2006 (http://www.girlpower.gov/adultswhocare/campinfo/hometown/quickstats.htm).

17. "Healthy Youth."

18. "Why Kids Join Gangs." Gangs and At-Risk Kids. January 1, 2000. Retrieved April 5, 2006 (http://gangsandkids.com/gwhyjoin.html).

19. "Youth Gangs." SafeYouth.org. Retrieved April 15, 2006 (http://www.safeyouth.org/script/teens/gang.asp).

20. "Teen Suicide Statistics, Signs and Facts." Family First Aid. 2004. Retrieved April 2, 2006 (http://www.familyfirstaid.org/suicide.html).

21. "Suicide." Teen Health, KidsHealth.org. March 2006. Retrieved April 2, 2006 (http://kidshealth.org/teen/your_mind/mental_health/suicide.html).

Chapter 7

1. David Elkind, *All Grown Up and No Place to Go: Teenagers in Crisis* (Reading, MA: Addison-Wesley Publishing Co., 1984), p. 192.
2. Karl Perera, "Self-Image—What Is It?" More-Selfesteem.com. Retrieved April 18, 2006 (http://www.more-selfesteem.com/selfimage.htm).
3. James Messina and Constance Messina, "Time Management for Recovery." *Tools for Coping with Life's Stressors.* Coping.org. 1999–2006. Retrieved April 18, 2006 (http://www.coping.org/selfesteem/lifestyle/time.htm).
4. Sally Byrne, "Coping with Stress." WholeFamily.com. Retrieved March 4. 2006 (http://www.wholefamily.com/aboutteensnow/feelings/stress/coping_tips.htm).
5. "How Much Sleep Do I Need?" Teen Health, KidsHealth.org. Retrieved April 19, 2006 (http://www.kidshealth.org/teen/your_body/take_care/how_much_sleep.html).

Chapter 8

1. Earl Hipp, *Fighting Invisible Tigers: A Stress Management Guide for Teens* (Minneapolis, MN: Free Spirit Publishing, Inc., 1995), pp. 39–40.
2. Donna Widener, interview. April 19, 2006.
3. "Teenage Brain: A Work in Progress." NIMH. 2001. Retrieved February 23, 2006 (http://www.nimh.nih.gov/publicat/teenbrain.cfm).

4. "Talking to Your Parents—or Other Adults."
Teen Health, KidsHealth.org. Retrieved April 19,
2006 (http://www.kidshealth.org/teens/
your_mind/families/talk_to_parents.html).

5. "What It Means to Be a Friend." Teen Health,
KidsHealth.org. 2005. Retrieved April 10, 2006
(http://www.kidshealth.org/teen/school_jobs/
school/friend_comments.html).

INDEX

A

B

C

ABOUT THE AUTHOR

Linda Bickerstaff, a retired general and peripheral vascular surgeon, writes from her home in Eugene, Oregon.

Photo Credits: Cover, p. 1 © www.istockphoto.com

Designer: Nelson Sá; Editor: Geeta Sobha